PATRICE GLENN

Interior Dialogue

Interior
Dialogue

Mary S. Myers

© 2005 Joseph R. Myers
4682 South NC Highway 150
Lexington, NC 27295
josrm@lexcominc.net
http://www.comdemco.com

ISBN No. 0-9657458-1-3

I believe that we all have interior dialogues, one way or another. I don't remember exactly when these dialogues began, but I am fairly certain it was after my first awareness of the Lord Jesus Christ as a very Real Person who loved me!

My first experience with Him was at a time when the circumstances of my life had literally brought me to my knees. My baby girl was about 18 months old. My sister-in-law had sent me a copy of the Methodist Church daily devotional, *The Upper Room*. On this special day, in desperation I picked up the devotional to read. I think it was January 26. I got no further than the verse that had been chosen for that day. It was John 3:3, where Jesus says to Nicodemus, ruler of the Jews, "You must be born again." I had seen that verse many times, but on this day I really saw it and believed it! But how could one be born again?

Well, for the next three days I searched for answers and asked questions. Then late one night I talked to a young Piedmont Bible School student who lived in the apartment next door. He read many scriptures to me but was not able to tell me how I could be born again at the age of 30. After my baby toddled over to get me, I went back to our apartment feeling comfortable with God, her little hand in mine and my hand in God's. We went to bed and fell asleep. Some time later I awoke, surrounded by the most wonderful sense of peace. There by my bed stood Jesus, holding my hand which had fallen off the bed. It was the first time in my life that I felt loved and I knew then, without a shadow of a doubt, that Jesus Loved me and that He always would.

When I awoke the next morning I *knew* that I had been "born again." My entire life changed. I began to have marvelous experiences and be led into the most amazing places during my dreams. That was when I began to have the Interior Dialogue.

After Joseph and I were married, occasionally I would share with him the Interior Dialogue. It was his suggestion that I should write some of them down for others to read. The following is a small selection from a great mountain of Dialogue.

—*Mary Myers*

As the soft sweet light of dawn
Slips thru my bedroom window,
Yesterday is gone.
A new day is born.
The silent Sentinels of the night
Stand by,
While from the throat
Of a single waking bird,
The first triumphant note is heard.
Echoing twitters rustle through
The leaves of each surrounding tree
As the small sounds of praise
Begin and swell,
Ending in a grand crescendo.
Softly stir the sleeping hearts below.
Soon they will arise anew
To find
That somewhere
Thru the hidden mystery of the night
Fresh seeds of hope
Have been implanted.

"Cast no reflection upon another
Even in thought…
If a wrong has been done you…
Remember it only as a
Misunderstanding…

For that is what it is…
And know that
It is for Me to correct…
And I WILL do that!

Love…yours and Mine…
Must be
Unconditional.
That's the only kind of
Love that there
Is."

At best we see only fragments
Of each other (or of ourselves)
That's truly what we are, fragments,
Cells in The Body and yet,
Taking a deeper look we see
Lying within each Soul
The complete One.
And remember He once said,
(In a conversation with His Father)
"A Body Thou has't prepared for Me."
It is then we know
He who made us
Made us for Himself
          To occupy.

"Bone of My Bone
          Flesh of My Flesh
I give expression of Myself
          In others to you so often
In the hope that you
          Will recognize Me and My Love
And need of you.
          Please respond to Me!
That we may unite
          And express our Love
In union to the World."

"Every moment that you are on the earth
Is for the conscious development of your awareness
Of Who I am and who you are.
I know you and call you by your name.
You must once again become aware of Who I am.
In that knowing you will gain once more
That consciousness that I Am is the Eternal You."

"In order to understand
These problems you are experiencing,
It is necessary that you learn to 'wait upon Me,'
Becoming conscious of My presence.
In the 'waiting upon Me'
Feel the soft winds of My breath
As I clear your mind
And sweep it clean of worldly tho'ts.
And then you will know in the 'Being still'
That I am with you
Here to Love and serve you."

"I will come to you in the fullness of time
When the day breaks in your heart
And the Son rises over your horizon."

"So, rest in Me,
Let Me express thru you
Who I am and who you are
And who all men are
Together — One in Being."

"In due season ye shall know the TRUTH,
Whom to know IS eternal life.
You will then know that I am redeeming
        Myself
In you — and that all are a part of Me."

"My resurrection was a drama,
A figment of the reality
Which can only take place in you."

"You can call yourself
 A poet, a musician, a writer,
 A millionaire...or an engineer...
 But...whatever you call yourself,
Remember that it all is only a part of Me...
 In calling yourself names
 Other than Mine,
You separate yourself from Me...
The separation, however,
 Being in your mind...never in Mine.
Remember that you are all a part
(only a part)
Of the Whole of My Being.
 Only in returning and resting in Me
Will you find the peaceful and harmonious
 Existence you seek.
So,
 Join with great gladness
 The free flow of the Universe.
 And know that it all...all
 Belongs to you...
 Through Me."

Once when feeling a sense of frustration
Over my inability to "do that I would do,"
I felt the Presence,
Heard His whisperings:

> "Don't you know there is never a moment
> When you are not under My command?
> You can no more elude Me
> Than your little finger
> Can divest itself of you,
> For you are bone of My bone
> And Flesh of My Flesh."

And once more my heart felt
The all-encompassing understanding
And consolation that only He can give.
And knew
That He who "hath begun a good work in me
Will finish it."
For that moment at least, I knew…
And when I think of it,
Tiny bits of realization seep into my heart again!

My soul is like a homing pigeon,
Consistently returning
To the Sanctuary of its beginning
Like the bird, as it zooms its way
Back into the Heart of God!

Oh, God, thank You for the Angels
You have given charge over my erring flights.
Cover me with Your Feathers.
Let me feel that underneath are Your
            everlasting arms.

"My Beloveds,
        Let there be no disappointment
        In your fellow man…for any weakness
        You may think you see.
        Rather know
        That I Am there
        In each one
        And…
        For God's Sake,
        Love Me,
        Recognize Me!"

I was walking
With two of my loved ones on a road
Leaving the city where we had just been,
Embarking upon a journey, the destination
Of which was to bring us together
With other loved ones from whom we'd been separated.
Joyfully we anticipated our walk.
As we were walking and talking,
A gentle Wind began to blow about my ankles.
It was familiar to me, that Wind.
At other times when I had felt it
There had been a sense of quickening expectancy.
But now I cried, "Oh, Lord, no — please no!"
Let me stay. Let me walk with them. Let me make
          this journey."

The Wind gathered momentum, engulfing me
          within Itself.
I was in the center of a whirlwind,
Being lifted higher and higher, sailing over the earth,
Casting longing, backward glances to my loved ones
On the path far below. I could see them no more,
But I felt them — felt their love
Which seemed almost to be new found,
As I remembered the plans we had made for
          our journey.
The Wind carried me on over the land that seemed
          familiar.
I could see rivers, lakes and fields
Canyons, mountains and valleys. The ocean looked
          smaller now.
I passed over some cities,
One that seemed to have a similar Spirit as that of
          Chicago,
Or was it Detroit?

I remember passing over huge railroad beds,
Terminals strangely still and unused.
In this city the Wind, which now seemed more like
        a Breath
Blowing me about, gently lowered me
Until for a time I was very near a woman walking
Along that street.
It surely must seem strange to her, I thought,
To have me gliding along beside her like this.
She gave no indication that she even noticed!
So, I passed on by her and in so doing had to duck
        my head
To miss the branches of a tree jutting over the walkway.
Turning around, I laughingly went by her again,
Saying as I did, "Didn't you notice that I am gliding
Beside you three feet above the sidewalk?"
Her reaction astonished me as she nodded
Without the slightest interest, saying,
"Yes, I saw you, but I am so busy thinking my thoughts
That it really doesn't matter to me."

The wind blew,
And again as at times before,
I felt myself being lifted.
I was on my way
Passing over cities and terrain unfamiliar.
Soon I came to a city like none I'd ever known.
I was allowed to descend, conscious now of
        touching earth.
Was it earth?
The people seemed like those who inhabited earth,
Yet they were different.

I approached some I saw in various gatherings
And began to ask questions.
"Is this St. Louis, Missouri?"
They laughed and replied, "What?"
"Well, then, is it Kansas City, Missouri?"
They laughed again and said,
"What is Kansas City, Missouri?"
"Oh, do please, tell me,
Is this the United States of America?"
They looked at each other and said,
"The United States of America? What is that?"
I began to wonder if I was on another planet,
When the Inner Knowing impressed upon
          my consciousness
That this was a part of that World Within,
The Eternal Now
That has no names and knows no boundaries.

I caught my breath again
In preparation for the continuing experience.
I found that I had been projected into space,
Into a beautiful all-pervading quietness,
A stillness so still, the like of which I'd never known.
It was all softly glittering,
Suspended like stars. Silently moving,
All of my former emotions were gone.
No fear or anxiety or concern existed here.
Like a baby in the womb of its Mother,
I knew the Presence.
I was in Him and of Him,
Thoughts penetrating my being
Pulsating from the Heart Beat of the Almighty.
Only two words were beaming themselves

Into my Consciousness from His,
"Trust Me!" Again the Great Heart beat,
"Trust Me!"
And that was all — the experience was completed.
The vivid dream experience
Was still with me, now a part of my very being,
My heart responding:
"Oh, Father-Mother God
Help me instantly to yield to Your slightest Breath,
To remain conscious of the warmth and
Great Love of Your Body."
And I was absorbed in the remembrance
Of the experience that had been mine;
Almighty God
Asking His embryo to trust Him!
I had had a transfusion of faith
From His Heart to mine.
In the days to come, I, too, like the Poet, can
"Push the grass apart
And lay my finger on Thine Heart."

"I came to redeem Myself in you.
I gave Myself to you
Fully expecting that Gift to return to Me.

I need you,
Must have you,
And will be made whole again
In and through you.

For you are a part of My very Being.
Made in MY Image?
Yes! Yes! Yes!

I gave the best that I had to you,
Myself!"

"While there is nothing that can draw you
From My embrace,
Yet, I am aware of the distractions
That draw your eyes from My Face!"

Lord, help me to understand Thee more!

> "Because of the involvement of your life
> With the souls of others,
> What I do now is an unlayering of your
>   consciousness.
> To do otherwise would be a forced entry of
>   Myself in you.
> Take care and KNOW that I Am with you."

He is reminding the listener
Of His promise:
"Blessed is he who shall hunger
And thirst for righteousness,
For he shall be filled."
He is saying,
"Because you are One of those
Who so hungers for My righteousness,
You SHALL be filled as you yield to Me,
You shall become a channel
Of my righteousness
>   For others."

"The very Heart of God cries out
For the companionship you seek.
Turn to Him and find it.
Then turn to the world — and give it."

"Would you go with Me to Gethsemane?
"Why, Lord?"
"To give back to Me the consciousness
Of My Being — in you."

"Yield to Me.
The fate of your whole world
Rests upon your willingness
To be My channel of Love.
Not that the progress of The World
Can be delayed or hindered
By your willingness or unwillingness,
But can you imagine what it would do for you
To be a part of this redemption!
        Think on these things."

"Your waiting has not been in vain.
If you will allow Me to break the chains
That bind Me within you,
All the desires of your soul will be manifested.
Believest thou not that I Am in you
And you are in Me?
I know your heart
And I promise you the Time will be shortened.
You will know My joy
And I will experience My joy IN you."

"You
          as My Emissary
Are a part of
          the first development
of Understanding
          of the actual Reality
of the Great Plan…
So,
          it IS vital to me
that You Know…
          of My great personal
                    Love for You…
You represent Me
          in All…
I must have
          the expression of MySelf…Now…
in You.

1. Last night I seemed to have a dream
Or a vision, I don't know which.

This morning as I think about it,
It still seems to be a part of those
Interior things that happen
To one when all the bars are down
And shadows are swept away.
As my thoughts return to it,
It returns vividly
As though repeating itself.

I remember sitting on the floor
With several of the Master's disciples
Around an old-fashioned wood stove.
They were not as we often think of them,
As characters in a play, but human beings
With characteristics and personalities
Like yours and mine.
There were no barriers between us.
We accepted one another whole heartedly…
Just as we were.

I think this is the thing that blessed me
Most at that time.
There were no facades, and yet,
Seeing each other as we really were,
There were also no criticisms,
Only perfect acceptance.
And The Master was also there with us
In His Own Loving Self.

I remember thinking: "How is it
That one may have a transforming experience
Upon personal contact with Him, and yet
Many do not have this experience,
Even tho' they may find themselves in
          His Presence?"

Inwardly a Voice began to explain to me
As tho' I'd spoken my thoughts aloud.
"That is true! Many have seen Him,
But very few…experience Him
Or come to KNOW Him
And this is why:

2. "We all see in Him what we wish to see!
Some see Him as a teacher,
Some see Him as a healing physician,
Some see Him simply as a fisherman.

And some see Him as an historical figure.
Some even see Him as a salesman.
And He IS to them what they see.
For they see Him in the light
In which they come to Him
And He gives to them what they seek.

Only those who come to Him
In utter self-denial,
Having lost all,
Coming altogether on their knees,
Not in the physical sense,
But in the heart, soul and body.
Only to these is He seen as Saviour.
And only to these
Comes that magnificent experience
Of knowing Who He really is.
And with this comes the deep inner peace,
The deep inner awareness
That come what may,
All is well.

For in this beautiful Man
One sees the perfect plan of God,
Experiencing then the reality
Of that magnetic Force in Him
As He draws all to Himself
Into the union and the fullness of that which was
In the beginning
When we all walked with God
And he saw what He had created
And pronounced it 'Good.'"

"Don't you know
That I recognize the difficulty
That you are having
In applying My Consciousness
That is in you
In your daily associations?
For so it is with Me.
But know this,
I do rely upon you."

"Hear Me crying in the wilderness of your heart.
Release Me! Let Me speak thru you
To the universe of My Own Being.
Let the longing of your heart,
My heart, express and answer My need,
My need for Love.
Oh, that you might know Me and My Love
For you, so that you might return that Love to Me!"

"You have been distraught only because you
Are conscious
Of your own beingness, not Mine—in you."

"My relationship with you
Is the same as with the whole Human Race
And that is
Individual, special, wholesomely
And spiritually yours.
I am dependent upon you, each one of you,
To help Me. Help Me to make that relationship known.
First of all,
My need for you is extremely personal.
That's the only way that the function of My Body, You,
Can be purified and brought into conscious existence,
That you can become aware of Me, aware of Me in
        each other.
But, of course, that awareness, as you know,
Must become very real to you.
Else, how can you make it known to others?
There are others like yourself,
Who occasionally listen to Me.
And as the barriers of their hearts melt,
You become aware not only of Me
But of one another and of the likeness
You have in common.
Then it is that you will release Me
Within Each Other. Do this!
Let Me come through!
Now is the time. Hear Me calling within.
And know that I Am. I Am. I Am!
And I love each of you.
How can I deny Myself in You?
We are together the Creators of the Universe.
The Universe within which you live,
I alone can live.
You are Me, My expression within this creation.
Release Me to live fully and freely within You."

Lord, help me to have the fulfillment
Of that portion of Thy Life that is mine
And I am made to live!
Give me wisdom and understanding
As I attempt to guide and direct
This precious one entrusted to me.
Help us both that our walk on earth
May be clear and balanced,
Not shaded.
Strengthen us that we may together
Climb to the plateau of Thy Love,
Drawing with us others
Who may be groping in the shadows.
Oh, Lord,
Let Thy radiance be seen.
We are in such need of Thee.
Our hearts do vacillate so
Between the unreal and the Real.
Lord, help us sink our roots down
Deep into the soil of Life,
That they may entwine the Rock
Of Thy Security.
Yes, Lord Mine,
Send rain to our roots,
Water my seed
And Thine!

"All that is, is Mine...
The universe, the warehouse, the storehouse,
All that is created.
All supply is flowing forth for every human need,
For every situation, and as it is released
Through you to whom it comes,
I can multiply it a thousand fold.
The supply only becomes yours when you
Hold on to it...then it becomes as stone...
Rocks in the pathway of your own progress.
Yet, this too, is a part of My Love for You,
For as it is written...
'Even the stones shall cry out witness of Me.'
And one day these very stones
Will magnify My Face and My Love to you!
So, clutch them to you...if you must...
Hold them very close...
For even there I am!
Even now they, too
Are joining in with the great Hosannah's
Of the released flow of the whole Universe,
For I Am in all things...even in You.
How can I tell you how much a part of Me you Are
Or how much I long for you
To once again know your own Divinity
And return to Me within You?

  The day will come when God Himself
  Will magnify Himself in You
  And the Trinity
  Will become One...
  Again!"

"Let Me have My Way
With you and know
That the victory is ours,
For so it has been decreed
Since the foundation of
What you think of as the World.
I will have My Way
For I have paid the price.
As for you.
Because you are willing,
That Price will be manifest,
Not because of you
But because of Me,
Because of My Love for you
And your response,
Which is My response
To My Love in you.
How can you resist Me,
Your Creator?
I can't resist you.
Trust Me! Trust Me!
I Am in you
And
You ARE in Me."

One afternoon
    While thinking about a troubled friend, I
    Dozed off and as I did...

    I suddenly saw myself standing at the edge
    Of a playground.
    The day was sunny with a strange brightness,
    Not like ordinary sunlight.
    Some children ran out to play.
    They were nude, and very clean.
    All of them were deformed.
    As I stood watching them, wanting to help them,
    Knowing I could not,
    I felt the Presence.
    He was standing slightly behind me,
    Very close to my right shoulder.
    I could not see Him.
    And then He touched me...gently
    And began to speak...softly.
    It was almost like thought transference.
    He said:
    "There isn't anything you can do to help them.
    They, like you, were created perfect,
    Born in My Image.
    The distortions you see,
    They alone brought about
    And only they can erase those distortions.
    Yet, they can, thru Me,
    Restore their perfect Image.
    You must work on your own Image.
    Walk before them.
    As you follow in My footsteps, KNOW
    They, too, will come after Me."

I awoke

> And almost still in that dream state found
> Myself saying, "Oh, there is nothing any
> Of us can do for anyone. Our work is on
> Ourselves! Each one of us owes to one
> Another that vision of the perfect Image,
> For we all were created
> In His image."

"There is no solidarity outside of Me.
I represent the Crucifixion AND the Redemption."

Disciple:

Thinking about many personal fallacies
With great trepidation.

Lord:

"If you can only accept yourself as I accept you,
And love yourself as I do,
Then everything else will fall away."

When you meditate upon just the two,
You and God in you,
God permeates your whole universe
And you disappear…and find there is only God.

"Accept yourself in My Love
And as you do this…you
Will find yourself
Accepting
Everyone in MY Love.

Only the Divine release of
My Love can allow you
To do this…thus
Conquering
All negative emotions."

"My Spirit is longing for your love.
Express it to Me, intimately,
And you will accomplish thru Me,
More that you ever hoped or dreamed."

"Your agony is not Mine.
My agony was
to set you free.
Sacrifice yourself
on your Cross
and set Me free
in you!"

"Separate yourself from your emotions
and
see each experience as progress
being made in the development of
all entities involved.
Know truly that I Am the Shepherd of
the whole human race
and
as such I am leading all of MySelf
into freedom…that is the freedom in
each of the expressions of My Divine Self,
of which you and all are an integral part.
I must and will redeem MySelf in each of you.
The most releasing thing that you can
experience is to rise above the ordinary…
the ordinary human emotions
and
allow Me to absorb, if you will,
all negativity…
So you can then express in the positive…
knowledge and understanding
of Who you are
and
Who I Am!"

"You will have to forgive My seeming inability
            to make Myself known to you…
That you may KNOW your omniscience
            in Me.
Know this
however,
            the Time is nigh
Even Now
            When all shall know
and shall understand
Who I am
In You
            and
In each other.

I will never leave you
            Nor will ever forsake you
And
This is for
            All eternity.

You are Me
and I Am
You (I will never deny Myself in you).

And such Is
The World.

All the Universe
is Me
and I
Must redeem Myself in all.

I need you...to do this.

You are Me
I Am you.
Let me have my Way
with you...

My Way?
That is My commitment
To redeem
the whole Universe."

"Days like this

                  are given to you

                              not because

I am testing you

                  but because you wish

                            to test yourself…

Remember in that testing…which seems always to be
unexpected…you NEVER fall short of My

                Understanding
…Your love for Me…needs no testing…

You are so hard on yourself…

            I love you…

                    relax and meet Me in every situation…

            THEN there will be no testing…

                  One day you will know Me…

                      Even as I know you…

for you will trust Me…even as I trust You.

                  And when this perfect trust in Me
           is established in you…
There will never be a need for you

                  to guard yourself against…anything
for then…you will know

           that all things are in Me…and I Am in ALL
and the perfect blending of Myself…in You…

                will take place…(as it will in ALL).
There is No fear…No Fear…

                whatsoever in Me…

                Know this…

        and relax

            in My LOVE…"

"Shed the web of the illusions
of the Not-self and walk in the
authority of Who You Are!"

"It is easy
　　　...a trap...
To be caught up in the earthly
personalities of one another
With little tho't of
Who you Are
　　　and Who I am
In All!

"Let this Mind be in you
　　　which was also in Me.
Have the realization of being,
each one, in the
Form of God...
And yet at the same Time...
realizing the need to submit
yourselves
To God...In each other...
and becoming obedient
To Him...
　　　Even unto the death...
that is in the Cross!"

"You can know of My Gethsemane prayer experience.
And you can know the victory that I knew
and know through it.
Truly, you are crucified with Me.
Nevertheless, you live
Because I live
and Because I live My Life in you,
All things are being made perfect in me...
Even you!"

"Know thee not...that I AM...
　　　　　and that that means...
　　　I am always with thee...
　　　　　　　There is never a moment that you
　　　　　　　　　are not under My supervision...
　　　You are My expression in the Earth
And as such...it is my interest, Love and intention
　　　　　　　to guard, protect & guide you.
Let Me have My Way with thee...
　　　Relax and bless thyself...
Realize, if you can, who you really are...and know that
　　　"I Am" is always with you...
　　　　　　Yea, you are a part of My Be-ing...
　　　Be-ing? Yes...for your Be-ing is My Be-ing."

"Come unto Me...and...the Truth shall
make you Free...for
I Am—the Way—the Truth—and the Life...
You must be willing to drop all of
your fantasies—all your
un-real imaginations—all that hurts

you

and

others

for

Nothing in Me hurts another—
Nothing in Me separates—
Nothing in Me will keep you from
Being Loved...So you must be willing to
Let Me heal you—
Heal you from yourself—
Heal you from your vain imaginations and
Bring you into the Light of
—My Own Radiant Self—
—which is You—
which is Your own Reality—for—
You are God!
Know this...Let Me reveal to you Who You Are—
Who I AM in You!"

"My Body…

        Has been severed…

      Remember…the portions? The segments?

You know the separation…

        Yet, you

           can be

                the cohesiveness

    between these individual portions…

You can

      Love…

        and

          You can Understand…

You can BE the instrument…

    Thru whom the transfusion…

               of the Blood…

      My Blood…IN you…

    that can & Will bring the healing

         of My Body…

My Body?…You…and all who now live…and are part

of the Universe, You ARE Me…Mine…My Body…

Let Me bring the Healing…of My Self thru You!

There IS no being on Earth…who is not a part of Me!

See Me…In all…Look deeply into My Eyes…

        You will find Me there!"

"Pride?
What is Pride?
It is the denial of Myself
in you!
The recognition of which
will bring to you
an awareness of Me in all.

Then,
What is pride?

Are you ready to have the cloak
of your pride pierced
That I may live again in you
a Loving and Redemptive Life
of realization of Myself in others
in you?

For God's Sake
humble yourself
to Me
In You!"

I had a soul
stirring…quick…intense…vivid…vision…
It was as tho' we were all in a school auditorium…and
having played our chosen parts…the day over…I saw
the stage empty…we, the actors, had finished the scene
for the day…and there…sitting on the stage…to the
side of it…was a Man…All Grace…Love…and
Authority…emanating from his relaxed, rather bent
forward figure… he was dressed completely…but
casually…in white…just pants and shirt…I could easily
see that He was lost in His contemplation of us…the
players…in His Love…I knew instinctively Who He
was…the great Teacher of life's drama…He'd just
given us full reign to do our own thing …to play it all
out…our own way…knowing full well…that He
Who'd set the pattern into our consciousness two
thousand years ago…that the magnetism…of that
great feat…and of the demonstrated Love of His Own
Heart…would eventually…but inescapably…bring
each of us into the recognition of Himself…in each
other. It was a deeply moving…unforgettable scene…
I can still see Him …sitting there…quietly…believing
in…all His majesty…

"Disassociate yourself from the foibles of
        your family…
Those relationships so meaningful to you…
and honor their struggle. They are struggling just as you.
Express to them the Love and Understanding that I
            express to You!"

"Accept the situation
Whatever it is
As My guidance for that moment
and for that situation
And in that way you can accept the people…or person
As being a part of My will and Being
No matter what is happening."

"Know Me as King
            in your heart…
And the Magi and the
            Kings of earth will come to you…
Bearing sweet incense…
                and gifts to Me…
                    in You!"

"**K**now...

    There is no facade
thru which My Spirit cannot penetrate.
See Me in all...

    In every person...
Regardless of the exterior that seemingly presents
itself to you.

    Know that I Am...and as such, I Am in all...
Longing to be released!

Take no tho't of the seeming complexities
of those who call Me by Name as their own.

    I Am...their own.
The great need today is acceptance and understanding of
    Me...In you and all whom you see!

The great need today is the total acceptance of
    one another.
With this acceptance comes total awareness that I AM...
In all...and of all.

Nothing is too much for thee...

    Oh! My beloved
Move into the freedom of My Spirit...

  The Spirit of *all* Creation...

    Creation which came into Being...*for* YOU!

Just as you recognize Me in thyself

    You must recognize Me in all.
My Continuance in all humanity depends upon this.

    My Beingness known by all..."

"My training for you
Now...in this Life
Is
   to have no reaction
            to sin...
But to see
         rather the
                  Soul of that entity...
The greater the sin...
               the greater the
         agony...
See rather
         ...Me
               On the Cross...
AND
         remember
               My Resurrection...
Now...let us
         Triumph
               Together...
         in *all* things!"

"There is a a great need for you
to realize Me in your Physical Body.
To recognize My Beingness
Within the miracle that is You.

Not just in the great mystery
that seems incomprehensible,
That is the eating, drinking, assimilating
and eliminating.
But in the miracle of it all.

The Body of Me that is you that is Me
Needs attention. Needs recognition.

Take this into consideration in your commitment
to Me
And know that the defilement of My Body
Which IS your Body, too
Is totally within your jurisdiction.

Purify the vessel,
The container
that you ask me to occupy,
The one you KNOW that I live in
and remember
The physical is Me, too.
It has to be.
It is My Creation
and I must have it
to Live!"

Lord, it is so difficult for me
because I am so sensitive!

"So am I.
But I can not lend My power
to personal attachments.

There is a difference between your personal attachments
and Mine;
In Me there is no individualism,
Only Oneness,
Oneness of the whole Human Race,
No difference.
Yield now to MY Spirit in you.
Let My tho'ts be yours.
You become One with Me
and let Me bring that Oneness to others
through you into the consciousness of all.
This requires the sacrifice of all you think
to be your own life
In order to make Way for me."

" Mind is the builder and
Mind is the destroyer…
So,
It is imperative to your life and Mine
That you Love…
Let this Mind be in you
Which operated in Christ Jesus.
Realize truly
That you are Me…My temple
And
Be ye transformed now
By the renewing of My Mind in you…
Submit
To the washing of the clean water…My word
Which is your Bread…
Bread of My Life,
Sustenance in you.
Eat
And become worthy to become
Who you are in Me,
I in you."

"Think of nothing else
except your relationship
with Me
and all else will fall
into place."

"Don't live in the sadness of
the moment...
but in the
Victory of the Ultimate...
We shall overcome
Each and Every One."

"You make the choice
and from that point on,
the choice controls the chooser.
None but you
can make that decision."

Once came the consolation
of His understanding
and empathy to me concerning my compassion
toward the suffering of this generation.

And He said:

"The sensitivity that you feel and experience
in the sufferings of others
is that of My Own Heart.
The anguish is from your heart,
Clouding your belief in the knowing
that all things do
work together for good.

I understand this,
Both your inability to know
and My ability to know.

Go with Me
again to the Cross
and SEE Me there.
Feel with Me
the piercing of My Side
and the flow of My Blood.
Experience the impregnation of MY Blood
as it fell drop by drop
Upon the Earth,
Leaving My Body
for yours.

Know you are Earth,

And know with Me
What I know.
Shout with me the great cry of Victory.
Know what it means, for it is so,
"IT IS FINISHED."
All pain, all suffering, all anguish...FINISHED!

See the beauty of the completed Work
in My Resurrection,
The rediscovery of GOD in You
In Me!"

"Perhaps it might help if when you are
experiencing anguish and anxieties
To think of it as unwillingness to trust Me
with these circumstances,
to know that I AM working out all things in
and through My Love
for each one."

Disciple upon seeing a
rather distressing situation
she could not control:

"That just frustrates
the hell out of me."

And after a quiet pause she heard,
"Would to God it did!"

(after tho'ts of envy!)

"For you…it is forbidden.

Blessed are the shall nots
for they shall.

Share it if you will
But my conversation is for you…
You!…All universe,
You!…My mouthpiece…My one
in whom I Am.

You have no message to bring
No responsibility to fulfill
Only the Being of Me
and My Love to all."

"Take no tho't of what you shall see
hear
or be.
Remember
All is a part of Me
Sink down...or rise up
            into the sweet quiet consciousness
                    of My Beingness
In all...
and realize truly...that I Am!"

"Suicide?
            What are you thinking of?
There IS no such thing as
        death...
You are a part of Me...
        and I Am
                Life...Eternal."

"Could you but see it
        There is a Light
on the Horizon.
It is the glimmering of
My Presence…
The soon to be
Promise of
My Beingness becoming
Manifest to *all* mankind.

Turn your inward eyes upon Me
and look
look again
into My Face
and know
that
I AM.

That…I Am…
and will bring the fullness
of the beauty of all My creation
into
the Consciousness of you
and the
Entire Universe.

Believest thou this?
      It is important to Me
Now
That you Believe.
Your faith in Me
      Can become
the generating factor
that is essential for the clarification
of all My Promises...

Let Me live
in you...
Let Me use you...
Allow Me to Be...
      In You..."

"There needs now
For you to have a clear understanding
of our Oneness
That is the knowing
of Me IN you...
and of
you in Me...
An awareness
of our personal and universal need
and use of each other...
Let Me continue to make this clear
to you...
Without Me
you can do nothing...
Yet in Me
All things are made possible."

"You are, none of you
        more important to Me
than any other...
        While there may be
a greater awareness
of Who you Are
        and Who I Am
in You...
There is
in My Heart
        No difference
        in the function
of My need
        in My Body...of You.

Each One of You
        Is of singular importance
In the ability of My Person
To manifest the Love
        of God...
                To all Mankind."

"The food that is moving
through your body
is like the thoughts
moving through your mind
(some nourishes, some does not).
Treat it that way and
flush it out…
Go to the springhead,
the clear water of My Word
and be cleansed
and renewed
by the washing thereof.
Stand
under the sweet fountain
of it.
Let Me
revive you."

"Your existence in this life
is so ordered
that you are locked into the circumstances
of the world...
Let me help you break the barriers
that surround you
and make Myself available
to you on demand...
I am aware of the Spiritual chaos and
confusion in the earth's atmosphere...
However, I am also aware
that My strength is made perfect in you...
Come as a little child...
        My child...and trust in Me..."

⬳

"Recognize Me
        in each one of you
and
recognize
the difficulty
        that I am having
in experiencing
Myself in each
of you...
Give Me the liberty Now
In the expression of My Creative Beingness
        In and thru you and all."

⬳

"In order to understand and dispense with these
seemingly problematical complexities you are seeing
and experiencing in human nature...It is important that
you 'wait upon Me'...conscious of My Presence...
and listening to My Voice!
Then you will understand...and be a channel
of My Love.

In the 'waiting upon Me'...there needs/must be a
clearance of your mind of all interference in the tho't
world...just simpy 'being still...and knowing.'
For I Am here...here to Love and serve you!
So 'Be still and Know!'

My Spirit is starving for the breath of your Love...
Express it to me...in the One on one ...and you will
accomplish thru me...all that you have hoped and
dreamed of...You will remember that I once
said to you...
'You are never alone...I Am always with you.'
Believest thou this?"

"In the recollection of your Childhood
experiences, know that they were ordained
by Me for the spiritual development
of all with whom your life is intertwined.
Your beginnings and endings are in My Hands.
Trust Me as I trust you.

Let there be no sadness in your recall
and know that I am in the refining fire,
bringing forth Myself in My beloveds,
of which you are one. I can say to you
now, in you I Am well pleased. So take
heart and serve with Me the redemptive
purpose of our Father.

It is true I did cry, 'I thirst' yet
I also said come unto Me and drink
for I Am, as are you, the Living Water,
as well as the Life within each and every one.
Be the cup now that holds that Water
to prime the pump, least it go dry.
And hear My cry again in all directions,
'I thirst'
and offer Me the water!"

Lord to disciple:

"You must
stop placing
such restrictions
on those
          whom
you will receive
and those
whom you
will not receive.
Remember…
I receive
them…all!
No questions!"

⁕

"My Beingness in you
          Is dependent upon your
                    Beingness in Me…
Long ago you made a
          commitment to Me and
I honor that commitment.
Thus it is that My Honor of you
          Brings forth
                    My Honor IN you!"

⁕

"What do you Mean,
>Who cares for you?...
>>I care...
>But more than that
>>When I faced the Cross
>I knew that I had
>>but few followers or supporters...
>Nevertheless,
>>I also knew
>>that I had a Divine commission
>to which my obedience would
>>save the whole universe.
>So,
>>it is with you...
>synchronize your consciousness with Mine.
>>Realize the purpose of our existence...
>allow Me to Be Myself in you...
>and forget who you think you are
>>and begin to know
>>and in the knowing...
>You will allow Me
>>to live My Life IN you...
>and YOU will then KNOW
>>Who you are and Who
>>I am
>>>in you...
>For we are
>>One...
>>the creator of all!
>>belonging to all...
>>and being All!"

"You will know Him…when you see Him…for you
    shall be like Him…
For He is in you AND He IS You.
So…Bless the Lord with ALL Your might…honor Him
    & Glorify Him within yourselves.
You must begin to recognize WHO you ARE…and to
    KNOW your true Identity.
Of course, therein lies the key
to your understanding of one another
That you might know Him WITHIN your own beings.
The time is drawing nigh…
There MUST be the recognition of Who I Am WITHIN
Each Being…For I Am WITHIN Each One of you.
Difficult as this may seem to you…
it is only a matter of pride
that causes the separation…arrogance & pride.
THIS is the source of the Fall.

Now is the time to protect each other…You can do this
by My Love…By understanding one another…by
accepting the failings in each other…For all is a part of
the Whole…The lack of Understanding of this…The
lack of recognition and honor and love and concern for
one another in Me is abhorrent to Me…and not that
which brings about Unity of My Being…
Oh! No! Each of you seem…Yeah, are intent upon
expressing WHO You are…
Not WHO I Am…in you…
and this expressing of self
can only end in My delay In and Thru each
one of You…

I beseech you, therefore My Beloved...to submit
yourself...
to Me and the expression of My Love to You...
which is the only cohesive Force on earth...
The expression of Me within each one of you...
Thereby moving into place the members of My
Body...
Bringing about the Fulfillment of My promises
to All Mankind..."

"Bricklayers
in the Temple of the Lord
Helping to prepare
the Place of
Worship for the entire
Body...
Can you be content to
occupy
Until you can
Become aware
of what we are doing
Together...
Can you submit to this
and to My need of you...
In order to bring into
fruition
My Promises...
To You?"

Disciple to the Lord:

"Lord, we are so mindful of You…and our relationship
to You and to one another…teach us…and help us to
understand how we may become more conscious of Your
Beingness in all humanity…and of our total dependency
upon Thee…in each other!
Oh, God…help us!"

Lord:
"What you must understand is that there is no person
more important to Me than are you…Nor are you more
important to Me than any other single being…
Yet at the same time…you must recognize
how singularly I am dependent upon all…
for each one of us must function together…
must realize our own Oneness in Being…"

"A life of disobedience
leads to another life
to learn obedience…
to learn truly
the Law
makes one free."

"Never be shocked…Why should you?…of the seemingly gross actions of certain levels of your present-day society in Earth…

See it, if you will, Only as lower levels of Consciousness…those in the shadows of darkness…and See ME as the LIGHT of the World that I AM…and KNOW that my LIGHT…will draw them to Me…

All into My LOVE and Forgiveness: Let there be no sense of frustration OR condemnation in your heart…For such is Never of Me…Understand, Empathize…and LOVE…Knowing that

I AM always 'standing in the shadows keeping watch ABOVE My Own!'

Join Me in My redemptive Love…For ALL are ONE… and there is no difference…I came in physical form…that ALL might be brought into the Glory of Our Father's Presence…and SO it will be!"

⚜

"There is no personal relationship that you can make with another…
Other than Me…
And I choose to seclude Myself
So that you may seek Me…
And know
that as you seek Me
I will be found of you…
In you."

⚜

"Take heart,

    there is nothing lost in you...

For,

    I have given you

        MySelf...

and Together we have

        the promise of

the Almighty God,

    Our Father,

that we WILL conquer.

You...

    are a link

        Between ME

            and Eternity...

And

    now...in the needed realization

that there IS no

        such thing as death...

May come the

    understanding...of

the Eternal Divinity

        and existence...

    truly...of Life...Eternal!"

"The connection
　　　　that you have
　　with Me
　　　　could be
　　　　　　　extremely unnerving
without the grounding that I
　　　　allow you to have with
the things of the Earth…
　　　　　　　Without this grounding
　　　in your present desire for
the expression of My Spirit
　　　within you…
You might possibly lose
　　　　the ability to be
　　　　　　　the channel of My Love
　　　　and of My Spirit
　　　that you are destined to be…
So,
　　　allow Me to have My Way with you…
　　　　and trust Me
　　　　　　to bring about
　　　the full redemption…not only of your Soul,
but that of all mankind,
And,
　　　do know
　　　　that I need you,
　　must have you…
　　　　for you
　　　　　　　and those who are also listening
are vital to the completion
　　　　of our Father's plan.

Remember, always…
        that I am…
and that I am
        with you…
                and will complete that which I have
        begun IN you…
You are a vital part of the
                Infinite plan for all mankind…
We need each other…I am giving My Life for You…
        and for Me!
There can be no separation…between us…
        We are One…You & Me."

"You can never be comfortable
in any situation when you expect
someone other than Myself
to minister unto you…
You, like Me, are here not to be ministered unto…
But rather to minister.
I create for you the very best
circumstances I can for your growth in consciousness…
Your awareness to become a real part of Me…
You are not a child…
You are My representative…
And I am now treating you as such.
The freedom that you long for
You already have…
Your only need is to recognize it
and to act upon it.
Do 'Be Happy' in Me!"

"There is no place on Earth
That is foreign to Me…
For all creation
Belongs to Me…
Is Mine
Through, first of all,
My own Creation…And
The promise of Our Father…
And through the act
Of My Redemption…"

"The world
  While a place of indescribable beauty,
  Pathos and suffering,
  Is also
And indeed, first of all,
  A place of circumstances,
  If not designed
  By our Father,
  Allowed by Him to come into existence.
For the cleansing and purifying
  Of the soul of Man,
That the knowledge
  And understanding of His Will
Might become the First choice of survival.
  That in that understanding
  Might come the realization
  Of where our Creation began.
And why!
  So,
  Learn of Me
  and of MY Love for you.
The battle
  Is that of the Mind.
It IS in the Thought World.
So, take the position
  Of Guardian Angel
  Over what enters your Mind.
  Use weapons readily at your disposal.
  Cover your Mind
  With the Helmet of Salvation
  And realize
  The Mind of Christ,
  My Mind,
  Is yours.
  I am
  Always near!"